Esmerie Amory

The Epistolary Flirt

In Four Exposures

Esmerie Amory

The Epistolary Flirt
In Four Exposures

ISBN/EAN: 9783337404123

Printed in Europe, USA, Canada, Australia, Japan

Cover: Foto ©Andreas Hilbeck / pixelio.de

More available books at **www.hansebooks.com**

THE EPISTOLARY FLIRT

THE
EPISTOLARY FLIRT

IN FOUR EXPOSURES

BY

ESMERIE AMORY

PERSONS OF THE PIECE.

ERNESTINE . . . *A woman who writes verses.*

IRWIN . . . . *A man who writes verse.*

PHILIP . . . *A man who writes poetry.*

THE EPISTOLARY FLIRT.

SCENE I.

Place: The library of a city house. *Present:* ERNESTINE and PHILIP. *Time:* Evening.

Philip.— How did it begin?

Ernestine. — How does anything begin, Philip? First the blade, then the ear. And the blade was such an innocent little green thing. Who could have dreamed that the full corn would be as heavy as this? [She lifts a large package of letters, and lets it drop to the floor.]

P. [looking about at the scattered missives].— All in your writing.

E.— All in my writing.

P.—What a pretty little field of corn it

makes.   I can almost hear the wind sigh
through the leaves.

E.— Oh, yes, the wind sighs through the
leaves — the wind sighs through the leaves.

P.— I 'll warrant that if you look within the
husk you 'll find as much milkiness and silki-
ness as — as Nature generally contrives to
create in such cases.   [He laughs.]   If I were
nearer to you I could read the address on the
envelopes.

E.— No one shall ever come near enough
for that.   [Picking the letters up and hastily
sorting them.]   Here you observe three piles,
containing respectively, four, twelve, and
thirty-seven letters.   The first were dated year
before last, the second last year, the third this
year.

P.— I understand.   Nature is never content
with mere geometrical progression.   And the

wind did not begin to sigh until there were enough leaves for it to sigh through. Suppose we start at year before last—before the sighing began.

E. [hastily glancing through the contents of the initial four].—Oh, there is nothing in them —nothing but gratitude and twaddle about myself. You know he believes that I am a poet.

P.—What a fool! You are a much finer thing: you are a woman.

E.—It does not seem very difficult to be a woman. I know many fellow-beings who are so distinguished.

P.—But the majority of them have miserably failed in the business of womanliness, a business in which you are a conspicuous success—in your way. But let us to the course of untrue love. Who was the first to write to which?

E.— He wrote to me first.   He happened to see a little love lyric of mine in a newspaper, and he wrote to say that he had marked it and sent it to his sweetheart, with the comment that it expressed his love for her more perfectly than he could.   That was all I heard of him for two years.   Then he wrote again, praising a triolet of mine he had seen in another paper.   He said I had done something never yet achieved — I had given a soul to a triolet.

P. [vehemently].— Never !   You'll find a box of figs growing on every thread of thistledown before you'll find a soul in a triolet.

E.— I perceive that you have not yet read *my* triolet.   Then he asked me as a fellow-writer to gratify his deep interest in my work by sending him more of it.

P.— And then you thanked him prettily,

and mailed him the best of your best, and he sent back superlatives.

E.— No, he did not deal in anything so cheap. He praised with discrimination; he condemned unsparingly ; he roundly denounced my careless workmanship, and extolled my tenderness.

P. [musingly].— Yes, your verse *has* tenderness — and that is something. Why, the average hand-painted poem in a magazine *could n't* be tender.

E.— Still, a trifle too much of feeling is a sickening thing. In my writing I never dare do more than merely hint at emotion.

P.— In your epistolary writing ?

E. [faintly blushing].— Oh, in my letters I'm afraid I show less respect for the artistic need of self-restraint.

P.— I remember. I remember.

E.— But you know I am not grossly definite. I hint and hint and hint as delicately as April hints of harvest.

P.— Ah, you have then become an adept in these six years. Read me some confirmatory extracts.

E.— In this first letter — the first one that he kept — I say, " I do not know how to thank you enough for all your generous kindness. To be so believed in would give voice and wings to a mute inglorious clod." That was after he had eulogized my rondeaus and characterized my sonnets by an adjective that kept me in the clouds for a week. After that he scolded me for my unhappy-go-lucky way of doing my work, and I began my next letter with, " Do believe me when I assure you that I shall revise and re-revise and re-re-revise. The fierce critical light that beats about my pen and ink shall not abate until I hear you exclaim, More matter with less art."

P.— And then ?

E.— Oh, then he told me he had called on an aunt of mine who had showed him my picture, and that it conflicted a little with his mental image of me. I *was* so flattered to know that he had had a mental image of me that I immediately called that an unfair advantage, and said that I had a large mental picture gallery of him, and that as it was very inconvenient to carry around such a collection of varying faces and forms, would he be so kind as to let me *see* one of his photographs. I should take very good care of it and return it promptly, unless I happened to discover that he had a spare one that I could keep. In that case I said I should put it in a very pretty frame on my writing table, and just below it should be these words copied from his last letter: "Your willingness to leave your work unperfected distresses me." What do you think happened next?

P.— He sent you his picture.

E.— He sent me *five* of his pictures, all taken at different times, and all within a year. "Vanity, thy name is man," was my first thought, and my second thought was, "What a beauty!" Of course I could keep only one of the photographs, and I chose the loveliest of all.

P.— Oh, admirer of beauty in man!

E.— I admire beauty in man, woman, child, beast, bird, and serpent. Everyone ought to be beautiful. Someone joggled Nature's elbow when she was making my face, otherwise my features would have been superbly regular. *You* told me that, you know.

P.—You have a superb figure. There is n't the faintest approach to a straight line in it. Like your mind, it beautifully illustrates the subtle forces of indirection.

E.— Oh, do n't, *do n't* say pretty things to me, Philip. From your lips they are such a pungent reminder of the flowers of yester-year.

P.— Did you tell your correspondent not to say pretty things to you ?

E.— I warned him that some of his expressions ministered to my love of the beautiful.

P.— And did you resist the temptation to say pretty things to him ?

E.— Resist the irresistible ! I found a belated November flower and pressed it and sent it to him. After his next letter, I say, " Your letter is a rich return for that fragile scrap of withered Novemberishness. The inspiration and encouragement that I am growing to de-

pend on so much come in so graceful a form
that the manner is worth almost more than the
matter." And next he hurt my feelings. I
sent him what *I* thought was a humorous piece,
and after criticising it severely he hoped that I
would not feel either hurt, offended, or disheartened by his comments. Here is my
response: "I *was* a little hurt ('unnatural'
and 'unworthy in every way' are 'words that
burn' in a sense that you could not have
intended), but I was n't the least bit offended,
and I am never disheartened." You see I am
reading you these bits from my letters to show
you the manner in which I revealed myself to
him.

P.—I understand. Innocent vision! He
was heart-broken over your hurt?

E.— He was a picturesque ruin. I could
almost see the moon rising over him.

P.— Ah ! It's not wise to gaze at that species of ruin by moonlight.

E.— Naturally I enjoyed his remorse — the real part, the exaggerated part, and the simulated part. I can't help liking a man who takes the trouble even to simulate an emotion for my sake.

P.— Can't help *liking* him ?

E.— Can't help liking him. [Sighing.] Oh, that was the period of sweet and innocent liking, before the miserable ecstasy began. [He laughs.] Don't laugh, Philip.

P.— Certainly the miserable ecstasy could be no laughing matter ; but isn't it extraordinary, Ernestine, the way that dread disease *will* pursue your flying footsteps ? There's an awful fatality about it. Do your very utmost to escape, and you simply *can't*.

2

E. [frowning].— That is n't a very nice speech.

P. [soothingly].— Oh, well, I was only joking when I made it.

E. [smiling].— If your insults were not so artistic I would never forgive you for them.

P.— As an artist I am not worthy to be mentioned with you. But what was the next step in the primrose path?

E.— Oh, then he fell ill, and I petted him a little. I said I would *try* not to worry about him, but that when his picture was standing directly before me several hours a day I could n't help seeing it, and to see it was to think about him, and to think about him was to be a little anxious — all that sort of thing, you know. In my next letter I say [reading]: " No, I cannot bring myself to send you one of my just-finished photographs. It looks so unhappy. And I am *never* unhappy — except when I have to have a picture taken. But I shall certainly frown as blackly at you as this picture does at me if you write me another letter in your present wretched state of health — no matter how short it is, nor how glad I may be to get it." Are n't you tired of all this?

P. — No, no. I came here to-night to listen to your writings, and to criticise them.

E. — But not my prose writings. Here is endless prattle about my verses and what he thinks of them, and his poetry, and what I think of it, the walks I take, the books I read, the people I meet, and — oh, yes, here is something more about his picture [reading]: " I brought back an armful of blossoming boughs from my walk yesterday, and wreathed a spray of wistaria vine about your picture. Only a few of its buds had opened, but in the night they all unfolded, and it dropped its weight of bloom down to your pictured shoulder. Was n't that a pretty achievement? And 't is my faith that every flower enjoys the — the influence it breathes. Do you still insist on my photograph? Consider! Friendship is a delicate thing. Why should I imperil ours by sending you the picture of a desperate creature, brought to bay by a photographer? How can I confront a soulless camera with my most soulful expression? How can I look at a speck on a wall as though it was the only speck on a wall that I ever loved?"

P.— What pretty little unconscious movements a moth can make in a resolute search after fire.

E.— About this time he told me he *loved* my letters, and that seemed a little presumptious, so I became a trifle cool; and then he

was very busy working on his novel, and I
did n't hear from him for weeks, and missed
him dreadfully. In explanation of his silence
he said that the heroine of his novel was a
somewhat idealized version of the girl he was
engaged to marry, and that as long as my letters were distracting his mind, this central
figure in his fiction showed a tendency to ex-
press herself in my turn of phrase, which was
utterly out of keeping with her subdued and
lamb-like character. I suspect his inamorata
must have been decidedly of the namby-pamby
order, or she could never have suggested a
heroine of that tiresome nature. However, I
constructed a reply in which wounded feeling,
gentle dignity, and a certain lady-like misgiving
each played a delicate part. I suggested that
our correspondence should cease, or at least be
suspended till the novel was finished. He flung

back impetuous sheets, declaring that he could not live without my letters. I assured him with entire equanimity that I was very certain he could. Then he plead with me. He said his novel sickened him to the point of tears; he hoped I would never mention it again. Poor fellow! he had reached the spot that every writer sooner or later is forced to cross — that deadly place where the heavens are brass, and the brain a broken ink-bottle, with only a thick, black smear where the fount of thought was wont to begin its easy flow. In a word, he had lost self-confidence. The girl of his choice was very kind to him. She thought kindness was what he needed. I knew better. I knew he needed to be flattered up to the skies.

P.— Trust you for a correct diagnosis!

E.— I quoted bits from his letters, and

praised their style and finish.   I had previously
extolled the few poems of his he had sent me,
so I had to find some new adjectives for them.
Then in desperation I recurred to his picture.
I said it was absurdly young and beautiful, and
that I knew it was vain, because it looked so
woe-begone when I neglected to dust it, and I
hinted that it was dusted pretty frequently, and
with my best lace handkerchief at that.   I
always spoke of it as " the pretty child," and
altogether I must have told him a lot of stuff
about it.

P.—What was your object in working his
picture so hard ?

E. [dropping her chin thoughtfully into her
upturned palms].— Oh, the pleasure of warm-
ing one's wings, I suppose, and the high moral
joy of teaching fire that all moths do n't get
burnt. My motive, I imagine, was one-fourth

flirtatiousness, one-fourth a wish to cheer him up, one-fourth curiosity to see how far he would go and one-fourth a desire to teach him the valuable lesson that it's wrong for a man to flirt.

P.— Each of you, then, really believed that the other was — hm. That is very interesting. And in return for this valuable lesson he probably taught you the equally valuable lesson that it's wrong for a woman to flirt.

E.— Yes, he did; and I needed it. He wrote me a letter that scared me a little, but I was reckless. I could n't help going on in the same strain.

P.— Poor moth! Poor moth!

E.— Oh, put your moth in the plural number. There were two of us, you know. Next he wrote me a passionate love-letter that horrified me. But on the last page his mood changed. He hinted ever so delicately that we were reeling, but that it was not yet too late to clear the mists and the delirium from our eyes — we had not yet spoken the words that kill. He begged me to help him to be strong — to keep him from becoming the man that I myself would despise. His letter was an impassioned confession of love, and an agonized entreaty to be delivered from it. Picture the state of mind I was in. Inevitably my conscience was sore, my vanity exultant, my self-respect humiliated, my heart inexpressibly stirred and saddened, my nobler nature wakened into vivid life ! That word " reeling " really stung. It pierced my leaden consciousness that the drama was to close. He thought I was " reeling," did he ? Very well ;

I would take steps to show him that my head was perfectly clear. This is what I wrote [reading] :

"Your last letter makes me exultantly happy. You are a good man — a good man, and a noble one. You stood the test magnificently. You *know* I did not deliberately set myself to test you — it was absolutely unintended — but it *was* a test nevertheless, and you came out of it like pure gold. You splendid fellow ! You don't know how glad I am. Because if you had been the least little bit *cheap* it would have hurt my ideal of you. And now the ideal isn't a particle hurt — it's glorified.

"It seems to me now that I've been a little merciless with you, and I've no defence except my love of play—of playing on an instrument as delicate and rare as the one I found to my hand. I wouldn't have cared to play with anything commoner. I can't plead ignorance, because, some weeks ago, I heard your voice through the air asking me if I knew what I was doing, and I answered back that I did know a little — and that I was shutting my eyes tightly to keep them from knowing more. And of course that is no excuse. You behold, then, a woman who confesses that she has led you on (though she did not mean you to go any further or fare any worse than you have done), and who is not altogether sorry, because it proved, what she suspected all along, that you are one of the very best of men. I honor you the more because the victory was not easy for you. If you had not been so sensitive and impressible, with such a capacity for enthusiasm and eagerness and sentiment and tenderness, I wouldn't have *wanted* to play. It was my consciousness of those qualities in you that made the pastime so pretty —and so cruel. Here is an excellent opportunity for me to despise myself, but — see how heroically I resist temptation ! — I am not going to do so. It would only make us both miserable.

" Do you know what will happen when we meet ? *I* know exactly. I shall be so overjoyed that all shyness and self-consciousness will be drowned in gladness. Perhaps my hands will shake a little, but that will pass in a moment or two. Then the thousands of things we want to say to each other will begin to crowd up, and we shall talk and talk and *talk*. In a few minutes we shall feel like disembodied intelligences. It will seem, to me at least, that every drop of blood in my body is in my head, and close to boiling point. I shall live more in an hour than I usually do in a year. I shall be perfectly happy. And if we talk for an hour it will take me at least four hours afterwards to realize that I have a body as well as a brain."

P.— Very well done — for a moth.

E.— I was crying my eyes out all the time I wrote it, but not a drop fell on the paper. It does n't do for tonics to be watery, and I meant that letter to be a tonic. He wrote back by the next mail, saying that I was no more a professional heart-tester than he was a professional pork-packer, and inquiring why I lied. I give it rather more plainly than he did, you know. That made me intensely angry, and equally determined to prove that I had told the truth. I mailed him a cold note, asking that my letters should be returned to me. He sent them back, and with them an impassioned appeal for my friendship, and I could not respond to that half-heartedly. Here is the last page of my reply [reading]: " I am sorry my last letter was cold. I let my hurt pride write it for me. But now that is all over. And I am coming back to you with all my heart, and looking straight in your eyes, and saying, 'Please do n't be troubled another moment, because we are going to be the truest and dearest friends forever and ever, and we are going to make our friendship the most beautiful and satisfying thing imaginable.'"

P.— And that is where you stand at present?

E.—Yes. And the important point on which I want your advice is this: The aunt of mine he spoke of has invited me to visit her. If I do he may possibly call on me. Would it be wise for me to accept the invitation?

P.— Oh, yes — yes! Everything that a moth does is wise.

E.— But we are on the solid basis of pure friendship.

P.— No doubt. But let me tell you something. The soul that sinneth, it shall die ; that is a heavy punishment. The soul that playeth at sin, it shall not be able to refrain from playing at sin; that is the insupportable penalty.

E. [reddening].— Bah !

P.— Good-by, dear innocent child. Your people are all abed, and I must steal out like a thief in the night. I am glad of your confidence, but — do n't let him talk to you — not just yet.

SCENE II.

Place : The parlor of a cottage on the lake shore. IRWIN sits waiting. He looks up as a rustle is heard on the stairs. Enter ERNESTINE.

Ernestine.— Oh, I am so glad to see you.

Irwin [with soft deliberation].— This is you — this is really Ernestine ?

E.— Yes. [She draws her hands from his clasp, and her eyes from his long gaze.]

I.— Of course I took the first train for the beach as soon as I heard of your arrival. I know it's unpardonably early.

E.— My aunt will be sorry to miss seeing you. She has just gone out.

I.— I am *very* sorry to miss your aunt. I

lay awake nearly all last night thinking of her.

E. [bridling].— My aunt is a very sweet woman, and a very beautiful woman. [Sighing] I — [stops as if confused].

I. — You have a — do let me say it — a beautiful figure [she blushes] and [with enthusiasm] the very loveliest color in the world.

E.— May heaven preserve my figure and my color !

I.— Heaven will be sure to hear that prayer.

E.— Why.

I. [with extended hands].— Because it is so near to you.   [In the lowest audible tone] Ernestine — Ernestine —

E. [as steps are heard without].— Is that the butcher ?   And Auntie *told* him not to come to the front door. Oh, no, it's the grocer's boy. He's going around to the back.

I. [turning to the window].— Any information regarding butchers and grocers gratefully received. [After a pause.] It is like dew upon the parched ground.

E.— Let us go down to the lake. It is too perfect a day to waste between four dull walls.

I.— There is a hammock out here under an apple-tree, with a big chair, and a book beside it. Let us go to the book of verse beneath a spreading bough.

E.— Very well.

I.— Or — I do n't know. I have a hammock at home, but no lake.

E. [impatiently].— Which shall it be ?

I. [leaning luxuriously back in his chair].— My dearest friend, the secret of happiness is to do nothing — except muse upon the delightful things that one might do.

3

E.— Ugh ! [She leaves the room, and returns equipped with hat, gloves, and sun umbrella]. Are you coming ?

I. [as they leave the house].— I am glad you made me come. I did n't know how heavenly it was out of doors.

E.— Has the weather changed so much in fifteen minutes ?

I.—Yes. You are with me now. [Tenderly] Ernestine, we are together. Do you realize it ?

E. [dreamily].— No, I can 't realize it, but it 's the loveliest thing in the world, is n't it, Irwin — our relation to each other ? It makes me so sorry for that gay party of people on the beach.

I.—Why ?

E.— Because all their friendships are prosaic. Ours is the only poetic friendship. But they would n't understand it if we explained it to them.

I.— No; but we do n't want them to understand. I am satisfied to know that every leaf and blade of grass is glad for us, and every wave is tranced in joy. Those enraptured woods beyond the lake understand us perfectly. Let us take a boat and go to them. [After they have pushed away from the shore.] There! now I can see you in a wide unpeopled frame of lake and sky. A person in a boat has the peculiar distinction of a passage torn from its context.

E.— I take all nature for my context. I belong out of doors.

I.— So do I. A primrose by the river's brim a yellow primrose is to me, and it is a thousand times more.

E.— I grew up in the heart of the country.

Think what a heavenly delight it was to be companioned from my earliest days by things that are not egotists, nor nervous, nor restless, nor unsatisfied, nor conscious of their bigness nor of their littleness, nor affected, nor garrulous, nor flurried. [Looking around.] Are n't we running into shore ?

I.— I want to get a nearer view of that curious tree. Do you know its name ?

E.— I know it by sight, but I do n't know its name. Names are an endless bother. I know very few of them.

I.—You do n't know the names of things you have grown up among ?

E.— No; I am intimately attached to the bones in my wrist, for example, but I do n't know their names. My appreciations of nature are infantile. I am an infant smiling in the sun, and with no language but a smile.

I.— Happy baby! It is permissible to caress babies.

E.— But not possible, thank goodness — in a boat.

I.—We are going into shore now.

E.—Why, no we're not. Those are not the enraptured woods you spoke of.

I.— No; these are merely ecstatic. You are right.

E. [as the boat is pushed up the beach].— I refuse to leave my seat.

I.— Ernestine, can't you trust me? Do you think I would give you even a glance of — of an unchivalrous kind?

E.— No, I should wrong you to doubt. [Going with him into the wood.] It *is* cooler in here, and you are flushed with that hard work in the hot sun. [They sit down with their backs against adjacent trees.]

I.— Shall we talk or be silent?

E.— I do n't know.   We are happy when we do n't speak, and not exactly unhappy when we do.

I.—Tell me about the " Pretty Child."   Is he good, or has he had to have his face turned to the wall again?

E.— How silly that sounds!

I.— That time you took him into the woods with you — carrying him under your cape, so that anyone you might meet would not know there were two of you — what a lovely time you had!   He leaned up against a tree and looked at you while you read in your book, and then a little wind roused him from his reverie and he flew off with the flying leaves, and when you rushed round to intercept his flight that same naughty wind flung him into your arms.

E. [with mortification].— Oh, I never said that last part. Never ! Never !

I.— But that was what you foresaw must happen.

E.—What nonsense ! If you are going to quote from those absurd letters of mine I shall go back to the boat.

I.— Never speak a word against those letters. No woman on earth ever wrote such letters to any man. No such appeals to the heart and imagination were ever made before, or will ever be made again. But why did you not return me mine ?

E.—Your letters seem ever so much more intimately my own than mine seem.

I.— How near we came to each other, darling Ernestine.

E.—Yes ; the only way for souls to get near

is for them to be far apart.   But you must n't
call me darling, Irwin.

I.—I did n't. I called you darling Ernestine.

E. [coloring].—You must n't.

I. [entreatingly].—Why not ?

E. [sadly].— It 's wrong.

I. [passionately].— No ; it 's right.

E. [looking down].— And I do n't like it.

I.—Yes, you do ; you like it better than
anything else.

E. [rising to her feet].— I am going back
to the boat now.

I.— No, you are not. You are going to
stay here forever with me.

E.— Dear Irwin, do be reasonable.

I.— It 's highly wrong for you to call me
" dear."   Besides, it 's improper, and I do n't
like it.   [Suddenly growing wistful.]   Am I
really dear to you ?

E.— Ah, do you need to ask?

I.—You treat me as if I were an ordinary acquaintance.

E. [looking at him with melting eyes].— Just a mere ordinary acquaintance — that's all you are.

I. [with his eyes on hers].— Darling, we are all alone.

E. [with mock fervor, as a picnic party comes in sight].— Darling, we are *not* all alone.

I. [after they are again in the boat].— It strikes me you look inexplicably happy.

E.— A woman's happiness consists in the kisses she does n't quite receive.

I.—Well, a man's happiness does not consist in giving the kisses that are not quite received. You might think of me.

E.— I do think of you part of the time.

I.— All of the time?

E.— Oh dear, no, Irwin. *Part* of my sleep is dreamless.

I.— And you think of me all the rest of the time?

E.— Not exactly *think* — that implies a voluntary action. But nearly every minute of my days and dreams has a sort of Irwinian flavor.

I.— Dear, I am so happy.

E.— So am I.

I.— But all the same I should like to throttle those picnicers. Why should mere picnicers go to the woods?

E.—Why, indeed? *They* have nothing to conceal. That is the beauty of prosaic friendship — it can be known and read of all men.

I.— Do you *like* to say things that hurt me?

E.— Oh, my dearest friend, your face is all

drawn with pain. What have I said? What are you thinking of?

I.— Dearest *friend* — ah! I am thinking of the girl I love — the girl to whom I have been engaged for five years.

E.— Do tell me about her. Is n't that her picture — that cardboard showing its edge from your pocket? Please let me see it. [As he reluctantly produces it.] Oh, Irwin, she is beautiful. Such sweetness, such candor, such a spring in the face.

I.— What do you mean by a spring in the face?

E.— Do n't you know? Why, elasticity — life — lift — *spring* — the thing that makes a tree different from a poem about a tree.

I. [resolutely].— She is to my life what the sky is to the earth — the heavenly part — the light, the warmth, the wonder, and the beauty.

[He replaces the picture in his breast, and folds his arms tenderly across it.]

E.— Is n't it time we were going home ?

I.— There are tears in your eyes, my dearest — friend.

E.— I am not your dearest.

I.— I meant to say " my dear."

E.— That is what the drummers say to the pretty waiter girls.

I.— Then I will say, " my dear child."

E.—That is what preachers call their wives.

I.—Will you let me call you " dear " without the drummerisque prefix ?

E.— That is better.   Still, it suggests the possibility of being made to feel cheap.

I.— Oh, Ernestine, I can 't bear to see the happy light go out of your eyes.   What is it that troubles you, sweet ?

E. — Only the pain that comes to those who feel too much.

I. — I know what it is — I know. It is cruelly hard. [His own eyes moisten.]

E. [bravely smiling]. — Not so hard as though we had nothing but — [pauses] ah — feeling — to comfort us. Why, we have unity of tastes and pursuits and interests, the materials out of which the tenderest and most exalted friendships are made. It would be shameful to degrade all the lovely possibilities of our intimacy to the level of a vulgar flirtation.

I. — You are a noble girl, and every syllable you say is truth. Here we are at our beloved woods again. Don't you enjoy them?

E. — Yes, I enjoy them, and I enjoy your enjoyment of them, and I enjoy their enjoyment of themselves. There is an effect I have often tried to get in my verses, and always failed.   Do you see that crumbling log lying in moss and ferns among its living brothers ? Does n't that suggest to you the deepest depth of repose ?

I.— I see what you mean.   The living tree has restfulness, the fallen tree more restfulness, the rotting log has reached the superlative of quiescence.

E.—You know my thought before I utter it.

I.— Do you think a mossy log is more reposeful than a grave ?

E.— Oh, yes ; a grave never was alive — it is only the covering of what once lived.

I.— Oh, dear !

E.— Are you grieving over the fact that you are mortal ?

I.—No ; I am repining at the discovery that the building at your left is not a hotel.   It is only a grocery. Do you suppose I could get anything eatable there ?

E.— Dried herring and sauerkraut.

I.— Ye gods ! Can two souls attuned to poesy subsist on herring and sauerkraut ?

E.— Do take me straight home, Irwin, and I 'll get you a charming little supper.

I.— No, I want to stay on the lake till the stars come out. I want to see your face by moonlight. [He springs to the dock, and returns soon after with numerous parcels.] Do you like to eat out of doors ?

E. [guardedly].— It depends largely on what there is to eat.

I.—When we get out of sight of shore I 'll show you.

E. [investigating the packages].—Crackers, of course, canned chicken and olives, some luscious ripe plums and bananas, and —what 's this ?   Ice cream !   Oh, you ridiculous boy !

I. [laying down his oars]. — There !   I did n't want to show to all the world around how two poets can eat when they do n't have to keep up appearances.   I 'll open that can. This chicken is the " piece of resistance," as the English boy said when he was translating a French description of a dinner table.

E.—What absurdity are you saying ?   Oh, Irwin, how sweet it is — this outdoor privacy, and the poetry of Nature redeeming even the prose of eating, and your adorable face so near — so near.

I. [putting his face nearer].— Darling !

E. [drawing back]. — And a newspaper tablecloth that *will* fly up at the corners.

I.— These bananas would be better with a rum sauce.   Do take another.   It does me good to see you eat. But do you know, I fancied that you always had a *delicate* appetite.

E.— How strange ! And I fancied that you always made *tactful* remarks.

I.— Have some more ice cream, Pussy ?

E.— Do n't call me by that horrid name !

I.— But you *are* a Pussy ; you 've just shown me the claws under the velvet.

E. [going into tears].— If you knew how I hated, *hated*, HATED cats, you could never, never —[she sobs].

I.— My own darling — friend. I am *so* sorry. You once told me so in a letter, and I was a fool to forget it. Do n't try to forgive me. I 'm an unfeeling boor. [After a sad pause.] Would you mind telling me your *favorite* animal ?

E. [sobbing quietly].—The porc—porc— porcupine.

4

I. [tragically].— Ah, I see you have not forgiven me.

E. [with a hysterical shriek of laughter].— Well, you *asked* me not to forgive you. And besides I *could n't* say chipmunk, though it really is my favorite, because then you'd think you'd have to *call* me that. "Come here, little Chip! Pretty little Chip! Chippie want an olive?" [Goes off into a fit of uncontrollable laughter.]

I.— Yes, I think on the whole you have rather more to laugh at than you had to cry for.

E.— Oh, Irwin, you must think me a frightful lunatic, but there's a reason for every bit of my lunacy. You see every moment of the sweetness and preciousness of this day is penetrated by the sharp sense that it's the last time — the last time. We must not meet again, and our letters will never be quite the same as

they were before we met. Then when you
hinted that about my appetite, it *hurt* me so to
think that anything not quite delicate was asso-
ciated with me in your mind, and at the mention
of that most loathed of all the animal creation I
could n't endure any more. But it is n't really
like me to be so foolish and hysterical, Irwin.
What makes me so silly when I am with you?

I.— You are not silly, darling. You are
admirably clear-headed and candid. See, the
stars are coming out. Let us pack the rest of
this stuff away, and give our last hour together
to heavenly thoughts and heavenly happiness.
Oh, what an accursed thing a boat is! No-
body can do anything he wants to do in it.

E.— What is it you want?

I.—I want to lie down with my head on a
fold of your gown, and look up at the near
lights in your face, and the far lights in the sky.

E.— How sweet ! But I 'm glad you can 't.

I.— I want to drink to the last drop the delicious cup of your nearness and dearness.

E.— Darling boy ! But I 'm *so* glad you can 't.

I.— I. wish that the joy of every lovely thing that nature has shown us, and every exquisite emotion that we have shown each other, should blend in our embrace. I want—

E.— Oh, good evening, Miss Tarville. How do you do, Mr. Sydenham. Yes, the water is delightfully smooth to-night. [In a lower tone, as the other boat sweeps past.] No, I do n't *think* they heard you, though that Tarville girl did have on her fathomless expression. But do be careful.

I.— I do n't want to be careful. I want to be reckless. Oh, the lovely moon in the sky, and the other moon in the lake. How happy they are ! Ernestine, Ernestine, the world is packed full, *full* of bliss.

E.— Irwin, that rum you did n't get on your bananas has gone to your head.

I.— Yes, the rum I did n't get, and the kisses I did n't get, and the caresses that never reached me — they 've all gone to my head, and to my heart.

E.— Those people are coming this way again. I daresay they do n't want to miss *any* of your conversation.

I.— Then I am going to take you home.

E.— Yes, do ; I am growing chilly. [He pulls silently to the beach. Arrived at the house, she takes a key from her bag and unlocks the door.]

I.— Why, is everyone out ?

E.— Auntie told me she would n't be back till late, and I gave the girl a holiday.

I. [entering with her].— Then we might have been here, blessedly alone, all this afternoon !

E. [opening her eyes wide].—Here ! *Here!* And lost the skies, and the woods, and the water, and the divine wind !

I.— Ah, sweet, no.   We should have had Love's deep, deep skies, and Love's flowering or flaming woods, and Love's intoxicating winds and delicious waves.   Do you love me, Ernestine ?

E.— Yes, Irwin.

I.— Then come.   [She goes to his arms and lays her cheek on his shoulder.]   This is what I have waited for all day — all my life. Are you happy, darling ?

E.— Not quite, dearest.

I.— But why — why are n't you happy ?

E.— You hold me too tightly — and you

hurt—hurt me, Irwin. That picture hurts me.

I.— The picture ? [He draws the photograph of his sweetheart from his breast pocket and sits down in stupefaction, gazing at it.]

E. [still standing].— What is it, Irwin ? Your face breaks my heart. Oh, *what* is it, darling ?

I. [groaning].— I am dishonored, stained, ruined ! I can never look my love in the pure eyes again. [He kisses the picture passionately, and the tears start to his eyes.] Oh, let me go ! let me go !

E. [very distinctly].— I am not preventing you.

I. [taking her hand austerely].— Good-by. You will tell your aunt from me how sorry I am not to see her. [*Exit* IRWIN.

SCENE III.

Place : The parlor of the lake cottage. *Time :*
Evening. IRWIN sits waiting as before.
Enter ERNESTINE. She is pale and cold.
He springs to his feet, and advances eagerly.

Irwin. — Oh, Ernestine, I thought you
would refuse to see me. I do n't deserve to
have you give me another glance after my
brutality in leaving you the way I did a week
ago. My heart has been aching horribly ever
since. I am so sorry — so despairingly sorry.
I have not the slightest claim on your forgive-
ness.

Ernestine.— I quite agree with you.

I.— But I could n't endure to part from you

in that way *forever*. [His lip trembles.] Won't you say you forgive me, Ernestine?

E.— Yes, I can say I forgive you. Sometimes I do n't mean what I say.

I.—And sometimes you feel a certain pleasure in saying things that wound me.

E.— Yes; that is precisely what I feel.

I.— I did not think you could be so petty.

E.— It seems that I can be.

I.— It is n't like you. It is utterly unworthy of you.

E.— Just as you please about that.

I. [after silently gazing at her].— I do n't understand it, Ernestine. You are not really the frozen creature that for some reason you are pretending to be.

E.— I will explain. When the tree is stark and cold the frost cannot hurt it. When it is warm with blossoms a lesser frost will turn it pitiable. When did Summer ever woo blighted blossoms into fresh bloom ?

I. [sadly].— Never.

E. [stonily].— There is no ripening time for our affection.   There is nothing after our blossom-time but death.

I.— But, Ernestine, even the sharpest spring frost leaves a few blossoms untouched — the petals of friendship hiding under the branches farthest from sun and chill.

E.— What do you want of my friendship ?

I. [bitterly].— Merely the assumption of civility accorded to an entire stranger.   After all, what unpardonable crime was it that I committed ?   I was suddenly conscience-stricken. Even the best of men are liable to be that. I tore myself from the brink of ruin.   Even an angel in human form might do that.

E. [with fire flashing through the frost].— There was no brink in the case. To suggest it is to suggest that I am not a good woman. How do you *dare* to say that?

I.— Ernestine, for heaven's sake, not so loud.

E.— Oh, my aunt is in bed with a villainous headache. Destiny has kindly arranged that I can be as loud or as low as I please. Brink me no brinks.

I.— I will never use that word again.

E.— It always reminds me of a shelving rock edging a pit. The poor fools above it are freezing to death, and despising the poor fools below. The poor fools below are burning to death, and despising the poor fools above. There is a picture of life for you! [Turning to the piano, and singing to her own accompaniment.]

Oh, the world is petrified
Hard with malice, scorn, and pride ;
Let your fallen brother slide —
While the days are going by.

I.— It gives me a little shock to hear you use slang.

E.— It would give you a larger shock to hear me use profanity. One completely overlooked advantage which a religious training bestows upon its possessor is the fine flavor it gives to such a poor overworked drudge of a word as damn. I once heard a minister tell a story in which that word occurred. He could not omit it — the very point of the story balanced on it. He approached it as though it might leave a black mark on his righteous lips, and in the very act of utterance he went all pink and tingling with the iniquitous joy of it. Now to a time-worn profligate that word is as flavorless as a slice of last week's loaf.

I. [wearily].— I suppose it is. Somehow I never pictured you as using either unkind, vulgar, or profane words.

E.— I suppose not. My own special aversion is for misapplied words. Once I wrote a thing that was n't a poem, though it looked like one. It was large, rough-hewn, grotesque, intense. I read it to a lady, who exclaimed, "How dainty!" It was about as dainty as a wounded bull charging into a football game. But "dainty" was the fashionable adjective of the moment, so of course it had to be used.

I.— Your anecdotes are extremely interesting, but they are not exactly what I came for.

E.— You came, I suppose, to say good-by; but [politely] I trust you are not thinking of going yet. It is scarcely eight o'clock.

I.— Ernestine, why do you hold me so aloof?

E. [laughing].—Why is the palace fenced with stone, and whence are garden walls?

I.— I do n't know what you mean.

E.— I mean that I am free! free! free! [She leaps to her feet and flings her arms outward with abandon.]   You have no longer any power over me.   I have purchased my liberty by a week of agony and tears.   One tender word would forge my chains again, and make them stronger than ever.   Am I likely to give it?   Or permit you to give it?   [She crosses the room and raises a window to cool the fire in her eyes and cheeks.]

I.— By Jove! you are beautiful to-night, with that freshness of color and intensity of emotion in your face.   You deserve to be free. Nature never meant you for a domestic woman — the type of woman who eternally looks as if she smelt the preserves burning.

E.— Yes, the preserves would be a bother; but what really, unfits me for domestic life is my incapacity for wrangling.

I.— Wrangling ?

E.— Oh, dissensions, contradictions, jarings, friction, discord. Did you ever visit in a house where the eyes of the wife did not at some moment in the conversation say to those of her husband, " Aha ! you see I am right, and you are wrong," or where the eyes of the husband did not say to those of the wife, "Aha, you see I am right, and you are wrong." Not to mention the horrible collisions with children and servants over every darn trifle that comes up every half minute of the day. I seldom pass a house when I am in a railway train without thinking, " The occupants of that house are wrangling and jangling each other's lives out. Poor devils ! Poor devils ! "

I.—I do n't like you to say "darn" and "devil."

E.—What do I care what you like?

I.—Do n't you care a straw for me, Ernestine?

E.—Divil a straw!

I.—You are reckless to-night, and wildly inconsistent.

E.—I am just what I happen to please to be.

I.—But if you are such a devotee of harmony, how does it come that you are discordant with me?

E.—I do n't know how it comes.

I.—Oh, be as perverse and heartless as you please.

E.—With pleasure. The only blessed are the truly heartless. It is not warmth in the heart that keeps one contented, but a constant little fire in the head. When I find myself

unhappy, I say, "Fool, you have been seeking
happiness in your feelings. Go find it in your
thoughts. Go build a little fire in your head."
You may have to toil and groan to get the fire
started, but when the brains begin to snap and
crackle, and fling out sparks — ah, the joy of
it ! You sit down luxuriously before the finest
and most expensive conflagration that earth
affords. Your hands and feet, your body and
soul, are alike glowing. Your happiness beg-
gars that of Paradise. You put some of that
costly fire into the poem or story you are making, and it will create responsive warmth, or
kindle a flame in minds most dull of burning.
Ah, Irwin, that is what life means — *not* the
satisfaction of the senses and affections — any
beast can achieve that ; but the satisfaction of
the angel that works in the brain and only asks
for a little fire to work with.

I. [fervidly].— Ernestine, you make every good impulse of my being thrill into fresh and splendid life. I am a nobler man for knowing you. Let us both keep alive that glorious little fire in the head. [Instinctively they rise and clasp hands.] We understand each other perfectly now. But how pale you look. You are exhausted. [Remorsefully.] I have tortured the noblest soul I ever knew.

E. [sinking down on the sofa beside him, and speaking with low-voiced energy].— I want to be always the noblest, the most truthful, the most inspiring woman you ever knew. I want to command the utmost best that is in you as unerringly as though I were a messenger of God standing in the sun, and speaking directly to you. [Reluctantly.] Some of my talk to you to-night was not truthful.

I. [kissing her hand reverently].— I know it, Ernestine.

E. [cradling the kissed hand against her bosom].—No, I pretended to be hard and flippant and vulgar and hateful to soothe my wounded self-love, and make it easier for us to walk on a crack.

I.— To walk on a crack ?

E.—Yes.   The straight and narrow path always reminds me of a crack.

I. [laughing softly]. — Ernestine, I feel almost light-headed in the joy of knowing that we understand each other perfectly at last. Even our parting will be robbed of its pangs, for, now that we can trust each other absolutely, we can dare to see each other again many, many times.

E. [with deep content]. — Yes; many,

many times. [They lean against the high back of the sofa, and exchange fond felicities with their eyes.] Oh, this sweet calm, how heavenly it is! [They gaze in rapturous silence for some moments.] · Dear, I'm *sorry* I was cruel to you an hour ago.

I.—Never think of it again. I knew it was only a little farce you were playing. [He puts his arm around her waist.]

E.— No, you must n't do that.

I. [penitently withdrawing it].— My arm had something to say to you. It wished to say that I forgive you for being cruel to me.

E. [with a humorous glint in her eyes].— I think — perhaps — it might be allowed to say that, providing — providing it does n't *stutter.* [He draws her closely to him. Her face is in his neck, his cheek on her brow. Suddenly she rouses with a laugh.]

I.— Do n't laugh.

E.— But I am thinking what an unfortunate person you are.

I.— In what way unfortunate ?

E.— You have two afflicted arms — one stutters and the other is dumb.

I. [rising to his feet and drawing her with both arms to his breast].— Oh, darling —

E. [in alarm].— Irwin, I never meant —

I. [fiercely].—I do n't care what you meant. Do you think I can stand your lips in my neck ? Do you think I can endure your warm body resting its tender weight on me ?   Do you think I can resist your seductive suggestions ?   No, by God ! I am not made of stone, nor yet of iron.   You shall do as I say.   You shall put your arms around my neck that way, and put your lips up to my lips this way [kissing her]. Oh, my sweet — my sweet —

E. [tearing herself from him in a tempest of tears].— Oh, Irwin, Irwin, Irwin, I am a vile creature; I am the weakest woman alive. Better make your best friend of some Magdalen than of me. She at least is what she professes to be. *She* does n't pose as your guardian angel, and your bright particular star. Oh, God help me! [She bows her face to her knees, and mutters a prayer amid her sobs.]

I. [with blank, colorless face].— My good Lord, how did we *get* to this state? Do n't cry, Ernestine, dear, do n't cry. What puzzles me is, how in the devil did we get in this pit?

E. [with averted eyes].— Merely by the action of moral gravitation. Let yourself go, and the greater the height from which you descend, the greater the velocity of your descent.

I. [with utter sadness]. — And we descended from such beautiful heights Ernestine.

E.— Oh, I know it! I know it! And we can never go back.

I.— Your defeat is not so terrible as mine. You are false only to yourself. I have spiritually outraged the woman who believes me true — the woman to whom I vowed my truth. Oh, Ernestine, I cannot tell you what that dear girl is to me. The very sight of her the day after I left you put me in an agony of self-contempt. She said she was glad I had taken a holiday, for I had needed it so badly, and she pitied me and petted me, while my guilty soul shrank and crouched in my body. I told her I had seen you, and that we had gone for a boat-ride, and that you were an interesting woman, and she said she was so glad that my holiday had not been a dull one. Oh, she stabbed me with her sweet lips, and I burned to tell her all—to hear her reproach, denounce, curse me — anything rather than believe in me. The precious girl! God knows I love her. There is nothing in my life that has not been opened to her eyes — nothing but this — and the burden of this false love, this secret blackness, is greater than I can bear. Your agony and tears have been matched by mine.

E. [weeping].— Irwin, why did you come to me again? It was a cruel parting — that last parting of ours — but it did not hurt as this does.

I.— Before heaven, I did not mean to tempt you, or put myself in the way of temptation. I wanted to *talk* to you again. It seemed years since I had heard you, laughed with you, looked at the roses in your cheeks. I could n't remember whether it was with me or with my picture that you had gone boating. It was your

sweet talk to the Pretty Child that first bowled
me over, Ernestine.   No man on earth could
have stood that.

E.—But, Irwin, I did n't think of the Pretty
Child as a man at all.   I called him by a dozen
pet names, and it always gave me a little shock
when you so easily took it for granted that
when I was talking to him I was thinking of
you.   And yet [sighing] I suppose it was your
existence and interest that gave color to my
fancies.   Oh, I should never have met you.

I.—Ah, my girl, my girl, we can never trust
each other again.

E.— No, I have lost your friendship forever, and all by my own imbecility.   Why did
I sit down beside you ?   Why could I not
have kept you at arms' length ?   [They look
at each other with unspeakable sadness.]   I
wish God would give me another chance.   He

trusted you to me twice, and twice I failed Him. Oh, I *wish* He would give me another chance! [They still prefer looking despairingly at each other to not looking at all.]

I.— Oh, Ernestine, if we only could by some superhuman resolution, superhumanly kept, preserve our beautiful companionship free from the slightest taint of passion. I cannot give you up. You are all the world to me. Must I give up all the world in order to save my own soul? I cannot believe it. We are rational creatures; we must regulate and control this hitherto unmanageable stream of tendency. Do people conclude to live without water because rivers overflow, and neighborhoods are swept away? No, by Jove! It would be degrading to have to admit to ourselves that we had not sufficient strength and self-control to govern a mere instinct of our nature.

E.— Ah, I do n't know. I have lost all faith. I am not wantonly wicked, but I have shown myself despicably weak.

I.— No, it is I who have been cowardly. I left all the burden of resistance with you. I will be strong now. Do you trust me, Ernestine?

E.— Yes.

I.— Then believe me when I say that I feel myself stronger now than ever before. Poor girl — poor weary child! I could gatner you to my breast as purely as if you were indeed a weary little child — just to see your dear face at rest before I go.

E.— Oh, Irwin, your eyes are full of the divinest tenderness.

I.— And my heart is full of the divinest ten-

derness. [In exquisite cadences.] Can't you
trust it, Ernestine ? Can't you trust me ? [He
draws her softly to him, and she drops her head
on his shoulder.] There ! now the little pained
crease is going away from between the brows ;
now the lips are taking their sweet curve again.
Close your eyes and rest, dear child. You have
nothing to fear.

E.— If I could only die now ! Die as the
trees die, slowly—oh, so slowly—and go from
rest to deeper rest, and through that to deepest
rest; and feel the ferns and mosses growing
about me — growing slowly, slowly, all about
me, amid the leaf shadows and the dew.

I.— And I should be there, too, darling.

E. [opening her eyes and smiling fondly].
— *You*, Irwin ! what should I do with you ?
Your warm look would wither my green ferns

—one shy sunbeam glance is enough for them.

I.—I must leave you now, dearest. It is so late.

E.— Not yet for a moment — just a little, little moment. [She gives her finger tips the pleasure of touching his face.]   I am so glad we are strong, and that we can trust each other.

I. [shivering].—Yes, I am so glad—*so glad*. Good-by, my — my own.   [Their lips meet, and cling in a long kiss.]   Ah, come closer to me, my sweet, my sweet. You gave me your soul in that kiss — give me yourself forever. You belong to me [huskily].   Nothing can come between us.

E.— Nothing but your sweetheart's face.

I. [with a groan].— Do n't talk to me of my pale love. She is my Bible — my heaven — my Judgment Day — my goodness-of-God in human form. But you are my *life*. I will not part with my life. Kiss me again, darling. Give me your soul — give me yourself.

E. [striving to free herself].— I will *not*. Let me go — instantly. Go away, Irwin — ever so far !

I. [holding her tightly].— Oh, you are virtuous ! You ! with your damnable caresses — your fingers on my face and your breath in my neck. You soul of a harlot in the body of a nun ! You spiritual prostitute clothed in ice ! You are not *wicked* — oh, no, you are only *weak*. Good God ! Give me a woman who *is* wicked and is *not* weak. Mud is lovelier than muddy snow. [Pushes her away, and rushes wildly out of the house.]

E. [following him and wreathing her arms about him in the starless darkness].— Irwin, I can never give you myself, but I shall give you the strongest love of my soul from eternity to eternity.

I. [putting her from him with soft-voiced and soft-gestured contempt].—Ah ! do n't — bother—me. Do n't—bother—me ! Do n't — do n't — *bother* — me. 　　　　　[*Exeunt.*

SCENE IV.

Place: The City Library.   *Time:* Evening.
PHILIP leaning back in a listening attitude.
ERNESTINE bending forward in an eagerly
speaking attitude.   As she finishes her nar-
ration she drops her head, half lifelessly, to
the cushions behind her.

Ernestine. — Those were his last words.
"Do n't — bother — me.   Do n't — do n't
— *bother* — me." They follow me always like
the dead face that follows a murderer.

Philip [meditatively].— H'm ; seems to be
a melodramatic cuss.   You have n't much
common sense, Ernestine.   That is why I
think you are not a poet.   Real poets are rich

in common sense. But. honestly, how much
of all this was put on ?

E. [sitting up straight with startled eyes].—
Put on ?

P.—Yes ; what hand is Imagination taking
in the game ? A hysterical woman is a very
deceitful creature, especially when she is mas-
querading in a man's form. In that case she
invariably thinks she is at the last gasp, when,
if the truth were fully known, she has not
ᵀeally arrived at the first gasp.

E. [sinking back wearily].— I do n't know
what you mean.

P.— In words of one syllable then. Is not.
your friend a fraud ?

E. [rising and pacing the floor].— Have I
told my story so badly as that ? He told me
the exact truth when he said that his life had
been absolutely pure — the exact truth when

6

he said that up to the time he concealed my
letters he had never concealed anything from
his sweetheart — the exact truth when he said
he suffered anguish because of this conceal-
ment.

P.— How do you *know* it was the exact
truth ?

E.— Oh, his eyes are pure as dew. When
did ever the eyes bear false witness ?   And
then he has the expressive face of a lovely soul.
Have you ever noticed that unlovely souls usually hide behind a face as expressionless as a
stone wall ?   I grew to learn so many of his
expressions : the sweet eagerness — the mirth-
ful look when he was making fun of me — the
contrite look when he was sorry he had made
fun of me—the look of quivering sensitiveness
— the look of yearning tenderness — the burning and broken look of passion — the gray look

of self-loathing and despair. Oh, he told the truth! His face and his voice and his eyes stabbed me with the truth. Would to God they had told me false!

P.— So then, as I understand it, this seraph with the seventeen halos is writhing in the burning marl of his own self-abhorrence. And all for what? All for a stolen kiss or two! Why, look you! I 've committed that same crime myself. I was a boy, and she was trailing clouds of glory as she came, according to my veracious fancy, and we were on the way back from singing-school when the awful deed was committed—and mightily disappointed she would have been if it had n't been committed.

E.— She would have honored you if you had n't.

P.— Honored me? Fiddlesticks! You never went to singing-school. And was I remorseful over it? Yes, I was. Remorseful that I hadn't kissed her again. Ah, the golden opportunities of youth! How shockingly they are wasted.

E.— What became of her?

P.— Oh, she married some honest John Tomkins, a hedger and ditcher. I meet her about once in two or three years, and it would do you good to see the sentimental look she gives me when honest John's back is turned. She thinks of course that I am consigning myself to perpetual bachelorhood for her sake, and I let her cherish the illusion. Rob a woman of her illusions and she wouldn't have charm enough left to mash an erotic maniac. Once when honest John's back wasn't turned quite far enough he caught me giving a sentimental look in response, and gracious! wasn't he pleased to think that I envied him his treasure.

It's the easiest thing in the world to make people happy. Be willing to humor their illusions, and they will steep you in perpetual smiles. Do n't you find it so ?

E.— Oh, forgive me — I was n't listening. I am in dreadful pain, Philip, dreadful pain — really and truly.

P.— My poor ingenuous child ! To think that had you been willing to marry me years ago — when I loved you — all this trouble would have been prevented. Or would it ?

E.— When you loved me ? Do n't you love me now ?

P. [smiling].— You can 't help being a woman, can you ? Why, yes, of course I love you now. I kicked the selfish part of my love out behind the ash barrel in the back yard of my consciousness, and framed the unselfish part in purple and gold — the gold of sunshine, and the purple of forget-me-nots. A feat that your seraphic friend does n't seem to have got the knack of.

E.— Oh, but I hindered him wofully by loving him all the time — yes, really I *did* — and showing him my love. And I helped you by never falling in love with you at all.

P.— That is true. Still, most men in my place would have scorned to subsist on friendship instead of luxuriating on love.

E.—Most men are fearful fools. What a blessing our life-long friendship has been to us. You were a dear boy not to let a one-sided love-affair break it up.

P. [with a masculine toss of the head].— And I won't be dear-boyed about it either.

E. [faintly smiling].—Well, you need n't be.

P.—I love to see you smile. Do you know why I have called your attention to the claims of friendship? It is to show you that love is not the finest thing in the world.

E.— No, the finest thing in the world is fame. That is the only thing worth while. That is what I shall live for.

P. [resignedly].— As I remarked before, you are deficient in common sense. What can fame do for you? Fame tears off the roof and turns the electric light on the family frying-pan. Fame strips off the clothing, and exposes the shrinking frame from triceps to tibia, while it calls upon the general public to observe that your spine is curly and your toes straight, or that your toes are curly and your spine straight. Fame is a thing of Roentgen rays — it pierces the flesh itself, and discloses the brain and nervous system as nakedly as a painted picture in a work on physiology. If I had a sister who was liable to become famous I should buy her the cutest little coffin you ever saw, and take the speediest legitimate means of inducting her into its mysteries.

E. [wearily].— Well, if it's as bad as that I shall have to content myself with being infamous.

P.— Ernestine! Why should you say that?

E.— Oh, I am in dreadful pain, Philip,— really and truly. If it were only my own pain I could bear it, but I feel the weight of his anguish pressing down on me — oh, awfully. Just as I felt his joy added to mine in the bliss of loving, so I feel his burden laid on my own in the weight of remorse. To be in hell is not the worst punishment. To know that I have dragged my child into hell — that is the unapproachable torture.

P.— Your child?

E.— Yes; he is my child. This misery-

stricken face that haunts me never existed until
I gave it birth.

P.— Please remember that, dear as he is to
you, you are equally dear to me. You are *my*
child, and I will not let you suffer.

E. [laughing hysterically].— Papa, I wish
you could relieve me of your grandchild. He's
getting too heavy for me to manage.

P.— Oh, he has n't manhood enough in
him to be *anybody's* grandchild. He is a wax
doll baby — ruined by the touch of fire. Ugh!
He makes me sick.

E.— The touch of fire did not ruin him,
any more than it ruined you and your school-
girl love. It was the touch of dishonor — the
loving two women when he had sworn to love
only one. He has the fiercely relentless conscience that makes one false step, or even the
cherished imagining of a false step, a blacker

stain in his eyes than the unpardonable sin would seem to another.

P.— Ah, I know the type. A moral Narcissus, soaked in self-love, self-pride, and self-righteousness, and accustomed to worship the image of his own perfections. Said he was humiliated, did n't he, and mourned over the flaw in his own immaculateness? I tell you I would rather be an ink-black scoundrel, oozing iniquity at every pore, than one of these self-righteous skunks that —

E.— Oh, peace! Perhaps he *was* a little vain of his moral superiorities. When they are less rare it will be easier for their possessors to be unconscious of them.

P.— And then his detestable selfishness! A really honorable man does not permit the wrong woman to fall in love with him. He freezes over, or forgets to write her more than a hurried note, or ignores her little coquetries. Instead of praising her for her pretty style of prancing over cantharides, he remembers how he would like to have his sister treated if she fell into eroticism, and restricts himself to generalities. This creature waits to see how far you will go, and then insults you for not going farther.

E.— Oh, he warned me — he warned me!

P.—When you seem helplessly in his power he begins to boohoo, not over *your* struggle and *your* tears, not over *your* aching heart and the hard, hard pain that you are so bravely enduring — no; but simply over the imaginary strain on his own selfish little lap-dog soul.

E.— I tell you he is not in the smallest degree to blame. It was I who brought him to this pass.

P. — What other pass could you have

brought him to that would have pleased him so well? Do you suppose he has grieved for a moment over the suffering that you had to endure? The rank egotist!

E.—Yes, he is an egotist — he is a man — it is the same thing. But all your denunciations are nothing but words. *I know him.* You would describe Eden by a minute account of the wilderness outside of it ; I have been on the other side of the wall. Nothing you or anyone could say would prevent me from seeing him as he is — the sensitive face, warm, keen, alive, intensely sympathetic, responding as vividly to my emotion as to his own — the lovely mirror of two souls; the eyes that caught me, and held me, and prayed to me, and caressed me, and shrank from me, and clung to me, and at last killed me with their misery — oh, the darling, *my* darling!

P.— He is not your darling — he is his sweetheart's darling.

E.— His sweetheart is perfect. Could she grudge me this drop from her full cup? I shall never write to him again—never see him again. She would not grudge me my little breath of life.

P.— So his *fiancé* is perfection, is she? I notice these desperately emotional, excitable fellows generally *do* marry a bread poultice, and endow it with the usual angelic attributes. [Rising.] Well, Ernestine, I can't help you, so I will leave you.

E. [entreatingly].— Oh, not yet. I want to talk to you about him. I love him so — really I *do*.

P. [comfortingly]. — Yes, dear, I know. And in six weeks you will wonder *why* you loved him; and in six months you will wonder *if* you loved him; and in six years you will wonder how he spells his name.

E. [scornfully].— That, I suppose, is the course of your love toward me.

P.— No; my love for you happened to be the noblest and finest thing in my nature, and it was transformed to a life-long pity for us. The love you feel for this outlaw is an illegitimate thing — it's a thing to be hidden in darkness, to be hinted at below the breath, to be thought of with shame. Reason enough why it should find a speedy death.

E.— Oh, I think it would pay me to keep it alive. It might prevent me from becoming a self-righteous pole-cat.

P.—Twist my words to suit yourself. You know —

E. [passionately]. — You have not the faintest conception of the sort of love I have for him. If he were so black a sinner that even God's love should falter toward him, my love would not falter; if the devastating years should rob him of all his grace and charm and vigor — make him physically an infant, and morally and mentally an idiot, my love would be only intensified. Did I not say truly when I said he is my child? Do n't you understand me, Philip? It is n't a matter of fancy or of choice — it is n't a matter of my wanting him to love me. I should rather he did *not* love me, because he would be happier that way.

P.—I have n't the least doubt that you think you are sincere.

E.— Oh, I *am* sincere, Philip. Every mood has its own sincerity. The trouble is, moods are such fickle things.

P.— You surprise me!

E.—Yes; there 's no knowing when they

will change.   And that makes people fancy you are not sincere [with a sad sigh].   Really, I am to be pitied.   I have two griefs.   Grief number one, because my lover has forsaken me, and grief number two, because grief number one is but mortal.

P.— I might endeavor to assuage one grief, but two is too many.   Shall I read aloud to you ?   Let me lend to the rhyme of the poet the beauty of my voice.   [Picks up a volume of poems, from which a sealed letter drops to the floor.]   Hullo ! here is a letter addressed to you.

E. [stretching out a languid hand].— Yes, it came this afternoon, but I did n't open it.   I was in no mood for ladyish twaddle and gossip in general.

P.— Perhaps you 'd better glance over it now.   *I've* tried answering unopened letters that were afterwards lost, and I never *could* decide as to whether congratulations or condolences were expected of me. Ernestine, what on earth is the matter ? You are deathly white.

E. [with forced calm].— She writes that cards are out for the wedding of — of the subjects of our conversation. They are to be married on Thursday.

P.— Well, you knew all along that they were engaged.

E.—Yes, but an engaged girl of five or six years' standing is such an old, old story. As a bride she won't be old at all. She 'll be new. Too suffocatingly new [groaning]. Think of the savage stab to my vanity.

P.—Yes; that certainly makes grief number three. I *thought* you could hardly escape with only two. And it 's worse than the others, because it 's in a vital spot.

E.—Yes, it's horrible.   And then, the indecency, the *immorality*, of it !   To be wedded to one woman in soul, and then go straightway off to marry another.

P.— Oh, well, it wasn't exactly your soul that he wanted.   At least, I inferred that from some things you said.

E. [rising with flashing eyes].— I wish her joy of him !   She'll soon sicken of his subterfuges and his selfishness, his contemptible crawling way of seeming to think of others' happiness when he is really caring only for his own, his disgusting habit of changing from flame to stone and from stone to flame at a moment's notice, his flippancy, his moral flimsiness, his —

P.— That's my brave Ernestine.   I can realize that *this* mood has its own sincerity.

Your words make grateful music in my ears. Let me go before they cease. [Closes the door behind him.] Pah! her disease has become tiresome; not interesting any more. Poor thing! A specimen for Nordau.

E. [going up-stairs].— If only my present rational state of mind would last! But it won't — it won't! [Reaching her room.] I feel it weakening every moment. [Seizing Irwin's picture.] Ah, darling, no other woman on earth could give you such a love as I could give you — so fond, so faithful, so self-sacrific-ing. But then [smiling at the picture through her tears], you know you do n't *deserve* a love like that, so an all-wise Providence is n't going to let you have it. Oh, dear! [Setting the picture down.] I do n't suppose I 'll ever find anyone else half so impressible as Irwin. Such men are all too few. No, I'll not cry. It will give me a headache, and I can't drive a head-ache away at the point of a pen as I can a heartache. Oh, how *desolate* I feel! [Flings herself on the bed in a paroxysm of tears.]

THE END.

PRINTED AT THE LAKESIDE PRESS
BY R. R. DONNELLEY AND SONS CO.
MDCCCXCVI

THE PUBLICATIONS OF
WAY AND WILLIAMS
CHICAGO ILLINOIS

CHICAGO
WAY & WILLIAMS
MDCCCXCVI

The Publications of
WAY AND WILLIAMS

AMORY (Esmerie).

THE EPISTOLARY FLIRT. A Story, in dramatic form, satirizing a certain sort of philandering men and women that abound in "literary circles." 16mo, cloth, gilt top, $1.

BAIN (R. Nisbet).

RUSSIAN FAIRY TALES. Illustrated by C. M. Gere. 8vo, ornamental cloth, gilt top, 264 pages, $1.50.

It is a reasonable presumption that curiosity will prompt many readers to inspect this volume, and it is quite as certain that those who read it will be well repaid.—*Chicago Evening Post.*

BARING-GOULD (S.).

OLD ENGLISH FAIRY TALES. With illustrations by F. D. Bedford. 8vo, 400 pages, cloth, $2.00.

The bare bones of these pretty traditions have been clothed in the flesh of poetic fancy and a charming and familiar style by Mr. Gould, who is now at the very height of his popularity as a writer.—*Cleveland World.*

BRIDGES (Robert).

ODE FOR THE BICENTENARY COMMEM-
ORATION OF HENRY PURCELL, with other
Poems and a Preface on the Musical Setting
of Poetry.   16mo, 54 pages, 75 cts.

*Two hundred copies on Van Gelder hand-made
paper for sale in America, $1.25 net.*

BROWNE (Francis F.).

VOLUNTEER GRAIN.   Poems.   Printed by
John Wilson & Son on Van Gelder paper.
Edition limited to 160 copies, of which 150
are for sale.   8vo, gilt top, 70 pages, $2.25
net.   *(Very few remain.)*

CHENEY (John Vance).

QUEEN HELEN AND OTHER POEMS. Printed
at the De Vinne Press on French hand-made
paper ; with vignette and headpiece reproduced
from compositions made by John Flaxman for
the Iliad of Homer.   Edition limited to 160
copies, of which 150 are for sale.   16mo, buckram, gilt top, 78 pages, $3.00 net.   *(Very few
remain.)*

CHESNEY (George Tomkyns).

THE BATTLE OF DORKING, the German
Conquest of England.   Reminiscences of a

volunteer, describing the arrival of the German Armada, the destruction of the British fleet, decisive battle of Dorking, the capture of London, downfall of the British Empire. 8vo, paper, 25 cts.; cloth, 50 cts.

COONLEY (Lydia Avery).

UNDER THE PINES AND OTHER VERSES. Printed from new type on deckle-edge paper. 16mo, cloth, 104 pages, $1.25.

DRACHMANN (Holger).

PAUL AND VIRGINIA OF A NORTHERN ZONE. A Romance translated from the Danish of Holger Drachmann, with introductory note by Mr. Francis F. Browne. Daintily printed and bound, cover design by Mr. Bruce Rogers. Gilt top, uncut, 208 pages, $1.25.

The voice of an artist, if not of a prophet, sounds from the North. . . . Wholesome, fresh, and elemental as the salt breezes it exhales from every page. —*Chicago Tribune.*

It is a pretty story of the Danish shore, of sand-dunes, coast-forests, sea-faring folk, and a boy-and-girl pair of lovers. To read it is to feel salt spray in the face and to breathe the fragrance of birch trees; to follow the sea in bitter earnest and to play with beetles in the woods; to make friends with rough, moody, kindly villagers, human and canine, and to watch the love of the blacksmith's bashful son and the Captain's teasing daughter through lyric childhood to dramatic culmination.—*The Nation*.

FRIEDMAN (I. K.).
THE LUCKY NUMBER. Cloth, 16mo, $1.25.

GARNETT (Richard).
THE TWILIGHT OF THE GODS. Cloth, 16mo. (*In preparation.*)

GISSING (George).
THE EMANCIPATED. A Novel. 8vo, cloth, 456 pages, $1.50.

HEMINGWAY (Percy).
THE HAPPY WANDERER. With title designed by Charles I. ffoulkes. Printed at the Chiswick Press on hand-made paper. Square 16mo, cloth, 75 pages, $1.50 net.

HENRY (Stuart).
HOURS WITH FAMOUS PARISIANS. Cloth, 16mo, $1.25. (*Ready in December.*)

HORTON (George).
CONSTANTINE. A Tale of Greece under King Otho. 16mo, cloth. (*In preparation.*)

HOUSMAN (Clemence).
THE WERE-WOLF. With title-page, cover

design, and illustrations by Laurence Housman. Square 16mo, 123 pages, $1.25.

The tale moves along with primitive directness and irresistible dramatic sweep, and the fascinated reader, impelled by the tragic interest of the story, lays not down the book until its fateful close.— *Dundee Advertiser.*

HOUSMAN (Laurence).

GREEN ARRAS. Poems. With title-page, cover, and illustrations by the author. 8vo, $1.50 net.

MATHEW (Frank).

THE WOOD OF THE BRAMBLES. This new Irish novel is a story of the Irish uprising in 1798, a most tragic period of Irish history, with all its exciting incidents of rapine and outrage and deeds of daring and self-sacrifice depicted in lurid colors. 8vo, cloth, 461 pages, $1.50.

MEYNELL (Alice).

THE COLOR OF LIFE. 12mo, cloth, 103 pages, $1.25. *(Second edition.)*

MUNKITTRICK (R. K.).

THE ACROBATIC MUSE. Humorous Poems. 16mo, cloth, $1.25.

NOBLE (James Ashcroft).

THE SONNET IN ENGLAND AND OTHER ESSAYS. Cloth, gilt top, 211 pages, $1.50.

NOEL (Hon. Roden).

MY SEA AND OTHER POSTHUMOUS POEMS. With an introduction by Stanley Addleshaw. Tastefully printed and bound, 76 pages, $1.25 net.

PAYNE (William Morton).

LITTLE LEADERS. A selection from editorial articles written for *The Dial* by Mr. W. M. Payne, Associate Editor. 16mo, cloth, gilt top, uncut, 278 pages, $1.50.

PEATTIE (Elia W.).

A MOUNTAIN WOMAN. With cover designed by Mr. Bruce Rogers, 16mo, cloth, gilt top, 251 pages, $1.25. *(Second edition.)*

ROSSETTI (Dante Gabriel).

HAND AND SOUL. By Dante Gabriel Rossetti. Reprinted from *The Germ* by Mr. William Morris, at the Kelmscott Press, in the "Golden" type, with a specially designed title-page and border, and in special binding 16mo, 525 paper copies printed, and 21 on vellum. 300 paper copies for America, of which a few remain for sale at $3.50 net. *(Vellum copies all sold.)*

SHARP (William).
Ecce Puella. 8vo, cloth, $1.25.

SHELLEY (Percy Bysshe).
The Banquet of Plato. A dainty reprint of Shelley's little-known translation of " The Banquet of Plato," prefaced by the Poet's fragmentary note on " The Symposium." Title-page and decorations by Mr. Bruce Rogers. 16mo, 126 pages, $1.50. Seventy-five copies on handmade paper, $3.00 net.

SNOW (Florence L.).
The Lamp of Gold. Printed at the De Vinne Press on French handmade paper. Title-page and cover designs by Mr. Edmund H. Garrett. 16mo, cloth, 121 pages, gilt top, $1.25.

One hundred numbered copies on Japan paper, with etched title-page, and in special binding. Price on application.

STODDART (Thomas T.).
The Death-Wake; or Lunacy. A Necromaunt in Three Chimeras. With an introduction by Mr. Andrew Lang. 16mo, 125 pages, cardinal buckram, $1.50 net.

TRAILL (H. D.).

FROM CAIRO TO THE SOUDAN FRONTIER. Cloth, 256 pages, $1.50.

TODHUNTER (John).

THREE IRISH BARDIC TALES, being Metrical Versions of the Three Tales known as The Three Sorrows of Story-Telling. Cloth, 160 pages, $1.50 net.

WATERLOO (Stanley).

AN ODD SITUATION. With introduction by Sir Walter Besant. Octavo, cloth, 240 pages, gilt top, $1.25.

WHITE (W. A.).

THE REAL ISSUE. Cloth, gilt top, $1.25.

WYNNE (Madelene Yale).

THE LITTLE ROOM AND OTHER STORIES. With cover design, frontispiece, and decorations by the author. 16mo, 144 pages, linen, gilt top, uncut, $1.25.

YALE (Catharine Brooks).

NIM AND CUM AND THE WONDERHEAD STORIES. Cover and decorations by Mr. Bruce Rogers. 16mo, linen, 126 pages, gilt top, uncut, $1.25.